# Kenta
## and
# The Big Wave

# Ruth Ohi

annick press
toronto + new york + vancouver

Annick Press Ltd.

We acknowledge the support of the Canada Council for the Arts, the Ontario Arts Council, and the Government of Canada through the Canada Book Fund (CBF) for our publishing activities.

**Cataloging in Publication**

Ohi, Ruth
    Kenta and the big wave / Ruth Ohi.

Issued also in electronic format.
ISBN 978-1-55451-577-6 (bound).—ISBN 978-1-55451-576-9 (pbk.)

    I. Title.

PS8579.H47K46 2013          jC813'.6          C2013-901206-0


Distributed in Canada by:
Firefly Books Ltd.
50 Staples Avenue, Unit 1
Richmond Hill, ON  L4B 0A7

Published in the U.S.A. by Annick Press (U.S.) Ltd.
Distributed in the U.S.A. by:
Firefly Books (U.S.) Inc.
P.O. Box 1338
Ellicott Station
Buffalo, NY  14205

Printed in China

Visit us at: www.annickpress.com
Visit Ruth Ohi at: www.ruthohi.com

*This book is for Naoyuki, Shoko, Masao, Leo, and my father, Fred Tsuneyoshi Ohi—with thanks for their time and care with Kenta.*

When Kenta heard the warning siren, he ran to school.
He ran to school like they had practiced before—
far up the hill, where the waves couldn't reach.

Then Kenta tripped, and his soccer ball did what balls do best—it bounced and bumped and rolled away.

The school gym was full of people looking for what they'd lost.
Kenta found his mother and father.

The ocean found Kenta's soccer ball.

Days later, when the ocean fell back to where it belonged, Kenta's family returned to their home.

"Everything . . . gone," said Kenta's mother.

"The house cannot be fixed," said Kenta's father. "It will have to be rebuilt."

Every night, Kenta's family ate and slept in the school gym.

And every day, Kenta and his
parents searched for what
the ocean had swept away.

Out of scraps, Kenta
managed to make
a new ball.

It was not the same, but it would do.

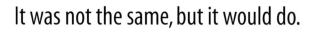

Not all things could be fixed so easily.

Out on the ocean, Kenta's soccer ball was plunged and pulled . . .

tossed and tumbled . . .

until Kenta's soccer ball found a beach . . .
and a boy found Kenta's soccer ball.

But the boy could not understand Kenta's writing.

So he found someone who could.
"This ball is far from home," said the librarian.

So the ball went into a box . . .

and into a truck ...

and onto a plane, which flew over the ocean . . .

to land on the other side.

And on Kenta's ball went, by tiny truck . . .

and bumpy bike . . .

all the way back to Kenta, who said,

"Thank you."

## Author's Note

In 2011, the largest tsunami (tsoo-nah-mee) in over 100 years hit the east coast of Japan. A tsunami is a huge wave caused by an earthquake or volcanic activity. The Japanese word "tsunami" means "harbor wave."

*Kenta and The Big Wave* is based on true stories reported in the news following the tsunami of 2011, about objects (some as big as motorcycles!) being swept away in the storm's waves and washing up on shore all the way on the other side of the world.

In Japan, earthquakes and tsunamis happen often enough that warning systems are in place and school children living near the sea practice tsunami drills—just like kids in North America practice fire drills.